Padma Shri Pran

Maurice Horn, the editor of World Encyclopedia of Comics, has described cartoonist PRAN as Walt Disney of India.

Entertaining generation after generation, his comics have been constant companion of all the growing youngers providing fun and amusement through his famous characters like CHACHA CHAUDHARY, SABU, SHRIMATIJI, PINKI, BILLOO, RAMAN etc. More than 600 of his titles are selling well in the market, and numerous comic strips are regularly appearing in various newspapers. His CHACHA CHAUDHARY comics had already been adapted for a TV Serial, and ran continuously for 600 episodes on a premier channel.

Travelling widely over the globe, he delivers lectures at various International Conferences. He has also been honoured with 'People of The Year Award' by Limca Book of Records for popularizing comics. His comic book 'United We Stand' was released in 1983 by the then Prime Minister Mrs. Indira Gandhi, and is still very popular among children.

Publisher

NOW THE MANAGER OF THE JAPANESE COMPANY MR. CHONGI CHO WILL SPEAK ABOUT IT.

PLEASE WELCOME MR. CHONGI CHO.
OH ! YA !

!!

OUR JAPANESE COMPANY WILL KEEP HELPING YOU LIKE THIS.
BULE TRAIN

BULE TRAIN
RIGHT NOW I'LL LEAVE.

TRAIN
I'VE GOT AN IMPORTANT WORK.
TRING !!
TRING !!
HI ! I'M CHACHA CHAUDHARY FROM INDIA. HOW ARE YOU?
CHACHAJI SPOKE ON THE PHONE FOR A WHILE.

.... AND THEN HE DIALED ANOTHER NUMBER...
I NEED YOU AND ROCKET.
LISTEN CAREFULLY,

OK, CHACHAJI. PLEASE TELL IN DETAIL.
OH, CHACHAJI ! HERE YOU ARE TALKING ON THE PHONE.

YOU'VE TO SHOW GREEN SIGNAL TO THE BULLET TRAIN.
PLEASE COME.
LET'S GO.
CLAPPING.
KRRIZ !!

KRRRZZ!!

IN THE MEANTIME.
BULLET TRAIN HAS STARTED.

IT WILL REACH HERE IN A FEW SECONDS.

WE WILL DO IT IN A MATTER OF SECONDS.
IT IS ENOUGH.

HERE I'LL PRESS THIS BUTTON ON THE REMOTE.

THERE THE BULLET TRAIN'S SPECIAL TRACK WILL BE BLOWN OFF AND THE TRAIN WILL BE SCATTERED LIKE A STACK OF CARDS.

OH ! I'VE PRESSED THE BUTTON BUT THE BOMB ON THE TRACK DIDN'T BLAST.
AND I'VE DIFFUSED THEM.
THIS IS SABU
BOMBS ARE DIFFUSED.
WHAT HAPPENED ?

YOU CAN CALL ME YOUR PROBLEM ALSO.
THUDD !!
BANG !!

I'LL RUN.

MR. JAPANESE, HOW CAN YOU ESCAPE FROM INDIANS ?
BANG !

WE DIDN'T DO ANYTHING.
YOU'RE THE CULPRIT FOR EVERYTHING. I SUSPECTED YOU WHEN...

..AT THE FUNCTION WHILE TALKING ON THE PHONE, YOU WERE SPEAKING IN JAPANESE, HENCE YOU THOUGHT THAT NO ONE WILL UNDER STAND.

BUT I HAD SUSPICIONS DUE TO YOUR EXPRESSIONS. WHEN I TRIED TO FOCUS, I UNDERSTOOD TWO WORDS.

IMMEDIATELY I CALLED UP A FRIEND LIVING IN JAPAN & ASKED HIM. HE TOLD ME THAT THERE'S GOING TO BE BLAST SOMEWHERE.
AFTER THIS, IT DIDN'T TAKE ME LONG TO MAKE OUT THE THREAT.
REST OF WAS TH RESULT (MY DEA ROCKET SPYING
NOW YOU TELL, WHY DID YOU DO THIS ?
OUR COMPANY MADE A CHEAP BULLET TRAIN.
BY BLASTING THE TRACK, WE WANTED TO PUT THE ENTIRE BLAME ON INDIA.
HOPE YOU WERE AWARE THAT IT ISN'T POSSIBLE WITH CHACHAJI AROUND..

8

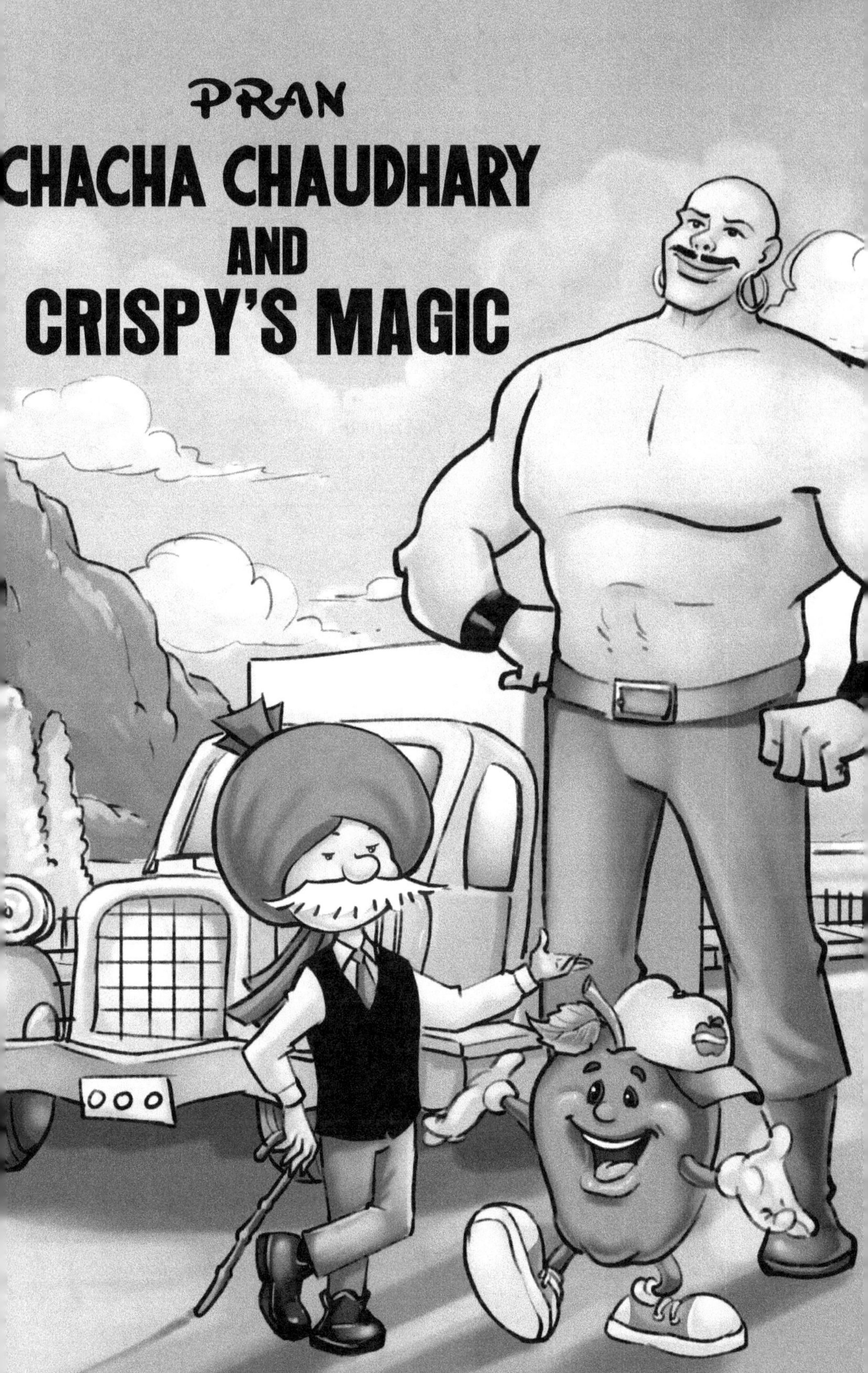
PRAN
CHACHA CHAUDHARY
AND
CRISPY'S MAGIC

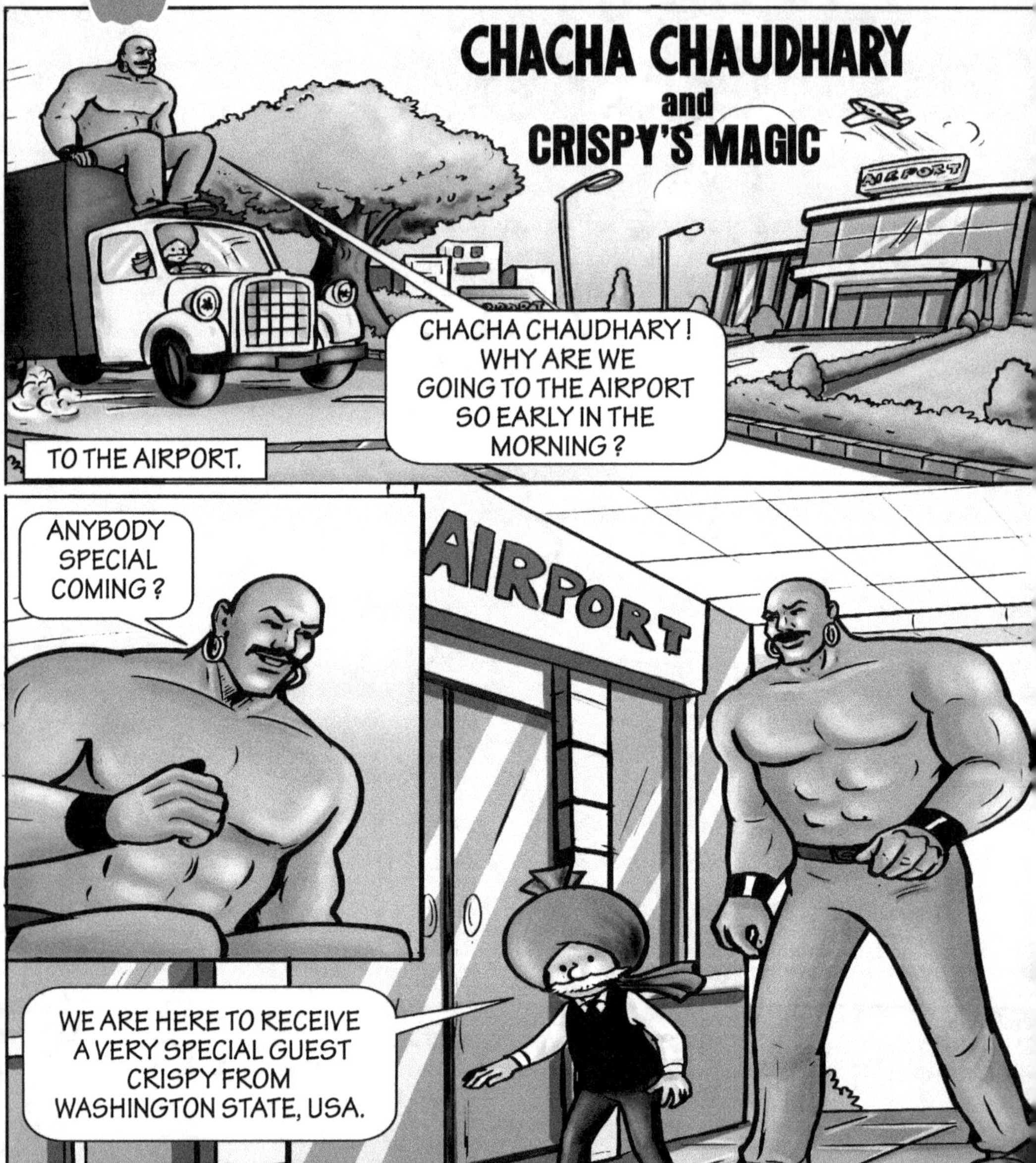

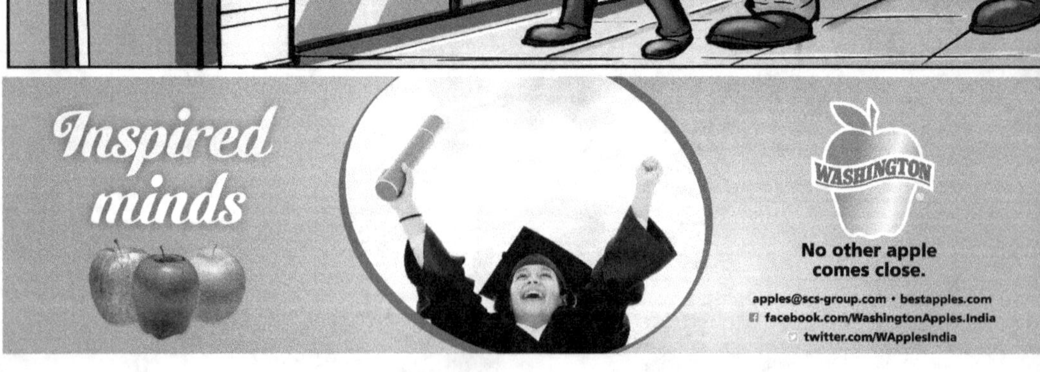

WASHINGTON

I'VE NEVER HEARD THIS NAME BEFORE.

WASHINGTON STATE PRODUCES THE BEST APPLES IN THE WORLD.

LOCATED IN THE PACIFIC NORTH WEST OF AMERICA, WASHINGTON APPLES HAVE MORE THAN 1,70,000 ACRE AREA WHERE THESE ARE GROWN.

HERE THE BEST APPLES OF DIFFERENT VARIETIES, TASTE, FLAVOUR AND COLOR ARE GROWN.

YOUR SECRET TO SHARP BRAIN IS AN APPLE A DAY.

3000 FT ABOVE THE SEA LEVEL, THEY ARE CULTIVATED WITH FRESH WATER RICH IN MINERALS.

Tasty delight

WASHINGTON

No other apple comes close.

apples@scs-group.com • bestapples.com
facebook.com/WashingtonApples.India
twitter.com/WApplesIndia

WASHINGTON

I'M ALREADY FEELING HUNGRY.
THERE'S OUR FRIEND CRISPY.
WELCOME TO INDIA.

Wholesome health

WASHINGTON
No other apple comes close.
apples@scs-group.com • bestapples.com
facebook.com/WashingtonApples.India
twitter.com/WApplesIndia

MY INTELLIGENCE SOURCES HAVE TOLD THAT CRISPY FROM AMERICA HAS COME TO INDIA.
IF WE KIDNAP HIM, WE CAN DEMAND A GOOD RANSOM.
HALT ! WE ARE GOING TO KIDNAP CRISPY.
WE'VE HEARD THAT YOU HAVE BROUGHT APPLES FROM WASHINGTON STATE.
THEY ARE AT BACK OF DUGDUG.

WASHINGTON

Washington Apples are a delicious source of dietary fiber which helps aid digestion and promotes weight loss.

HUBA... HUBBA!
SWOOSH!
THUD D !

OHH !
KICK K !
WHAM M !
OWWW !
WHERE HAVE THEY GONE ?
I'LL HAVE AN APPLE.
WELCOME TO INDIA, CRISPY.
DIRECT TO WASHINGTON STATE'S JAIL.

Washington
Apples

Wholesome health

Healthy eating doesn't get better than this.
Every bite of Washington apples is filled
with juicy goodness.
So go ahead, take another bite!

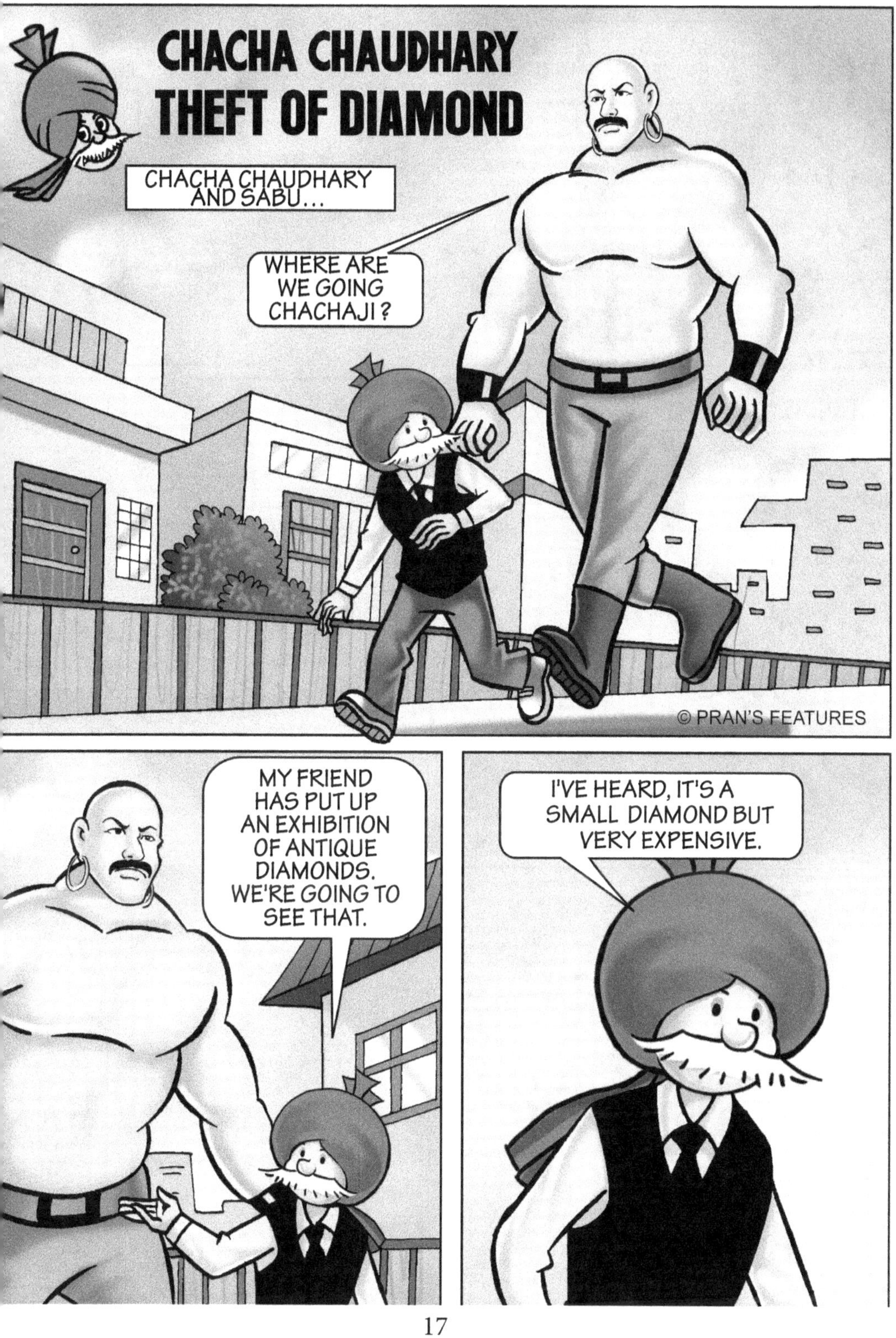

CHACHA CHAUDHARY
THEFT OF DIAMOND

WHAT WOULD BE ITS PRICE CHACHAJI ?
DON'T KNOW ?
I KNOW.
3 CRORE RUPEES.
I'LL STEAL THAT DIAMOND.
HOW JOMEO ? I'VE HEARD CHACHA CHAUDHARY WOULD BE THERE.
LET HIM BE. I'LL STEAL IT RIGHT IN FRONT OF HIS EYES & ESCAPE.

HA-HA-HA.

WELCOME CHACHAJI.
THANK YOU.

THIS IS THE DIAMOND - SMALL BUT EXQUISITE !!

IT'S GOT A STRANGE SHAPE.

COME CHACHAJI, TAKE SOME REFRESHMENT.

COME.

THEN.
OH!
OH! WHAT HAPPENED TO THE LIGHT?

SOMEONE SWITCH ON THE LIGHT.

THANK GOD! IT'S BACK.

WHERE'S THE DIAMOND?

DIAMOND IS STOLEN!
STOLEN!

NOBODY HAS GONE OUT AS YET. IT MEANS, THE DIAMOND THIEF WOULD BE HERE ONLY.

APOLOGIES ...BUT WE HAVE TO SEARCH EVERYONE.

NO PROBLEM.

NO ONE'S GOT THE DIAMOND.

STRANGE! THE DIAMOND HAS GOT STOLEN. NOBODY HAS LEFT FROM HERE AS YET.

IT MEANS BOTH, THE THIEF AND THE DIAMOND, ARE STILL HERE. BUT HOW TO SEARCH THEM?

EVERYONE COME OUT ONE BY ONE.

JUST WAIT. BEFORE LEAVING, PLEASE LISTEN TO A JOKE.

CHACHAJI, I'VE LOST A PRECIOUS DIAMOND & YOU'RE CRACKING JOKES & HAVING FUN?

YES! AND I'LL DEFINITELY CRACK JOKES.

SO FRIENDS, THE JOKE IS THAT A MAN GOES TO A DENTIST TO GET HIS TOOTH EXTRACTED.
THE DENTIST TOLD HIM TO OPEN HIS MOUTH. HE OPENED HIS MOUTH. BUT THE DENTIST TOLD HIM TO OPEN WIDER...
... HE DID THAT & THE DENTIST AGAIN REPEATED THE INSTRUCTION.
FINALLY THE MAN GOT IRRITATED. HE TOLD THE DENTIST...

... DOCTOR! DO YOU PLAN TO SIT IN MY MOUTH AND EXTRACT THE TOOTH? THAT'S WHY YOU SEEM TO GIVE ME THIS INSTRUCTION.

HA-HA-HA.

HA-HA !

THERE.

YOU STOP LAUGHING.
THUDD !!
OUCH !!

CHACHAJI ! WHY DID YOU HIT HIM ?

BECAUSE HE IS THE DIAMOND THIEF.

HE WAS HIDING THE DIAMOND IN HIS TOOTH.
HERE'S IT.

OUCH !!
!!
!!

YOU'RE AMAZING, CHACHAJI. HOW DID YOU MAKE THIS OUT ?
THE SHAPE OF DIAMOND WAS LIKE A TOOTH. THE THIEF ALSO NOTICED THAT. HENCE, HE TOOK BENEFIT OF THE DARKNESS AND FITTED IT INTO HIS BROKEN TEETH.

NOW I COULDN'T MAKE EVERYONE OPEN HIS MOUTH FOR THE CHECKING. SO I THOUGHT OF TELLING A JOKE.

SO, THE DIAMOND IS IN YOUR HANDS.*
* CHACHA CHAUDHARY'S BRAIN WORKS FASTER THAN A COMPUTER

CHACHA CHAUDHARY
FOREST FIRE

SABU! COME HERE.

WHAT'S THIS CHACHAJI?

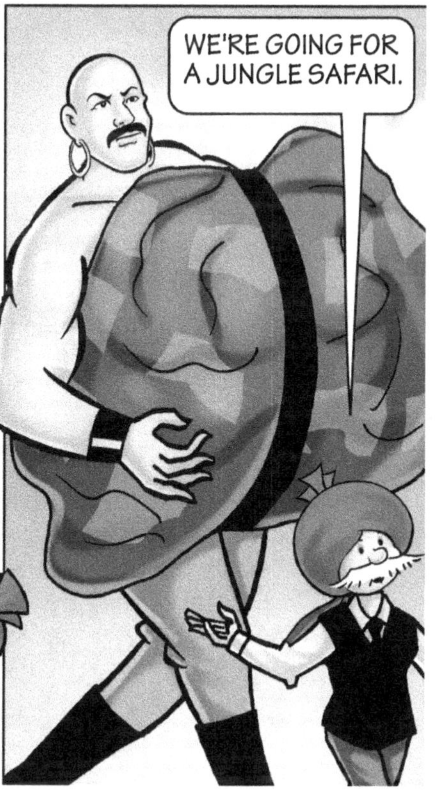

WE'RE GOING FOR A JUNGLE SAFARI.

THIS IS YOUR BED FOR THE SAFARI.
IT CAN BE BLOWN BY AIR.

JUST CHECK IT.
OK I'LL DO THAT.

SPLASH !!
SPLASH !!

IT'S OK.
OURS ALSO FINE.

GET READY. WE'RE LEAVING IN THE MORNING WITH A GROUP FOR JUNGLE SAFARI.

NEXT MORNING.

WOW! WHAT AN AMAZING FOREST...

BE CAREFUL OF THE WILD ANIMALS HERE.

CHACHIJI, IF YOU COME ACROSS A LION HERE, WHAT WILL YOU DO ?

WHAT WILL SHE DO ? SHE'LL JUST SCOLD HIM AND THE LION WILL BE SCARED AWAY.

REALLY !!
ABSOLUTELY ! WHEN YOUR CHACHA HAS A SIMILAR PLIGHT IN FRONT OF HER THEN ....

... POOR LION CAN'T BE SPARED.
HO-HO-HO !

AREN'T YOU SPEAKING A BIT TOO MUCH TODAY ?
O...OH !!

SUDDENLY.
RUN !
RUN !!

WHAT HAPPENED, WHY ARE THE NATIVES RUNNING LIKE THIS ?

FIRE ! THERE'S A FIRE IN THE JUNGLE.
OH !

OH !
OH !

THIS FOREST FIRE IS SCARY.
IT WILL KEEP ON INCREASING IF NOTHING IS DONE.
WHAT TO DO ? LOTS OF WATER IS REQUIRED FOR EXTINGUISHING IT.

WHERE CAN WE GET SO MUCH WATER FROM ?
WE'LL GET IT.

SABU ! YOUR AIR BED.

UNDERSTOOD CHACHAJI.

SPLASH!!

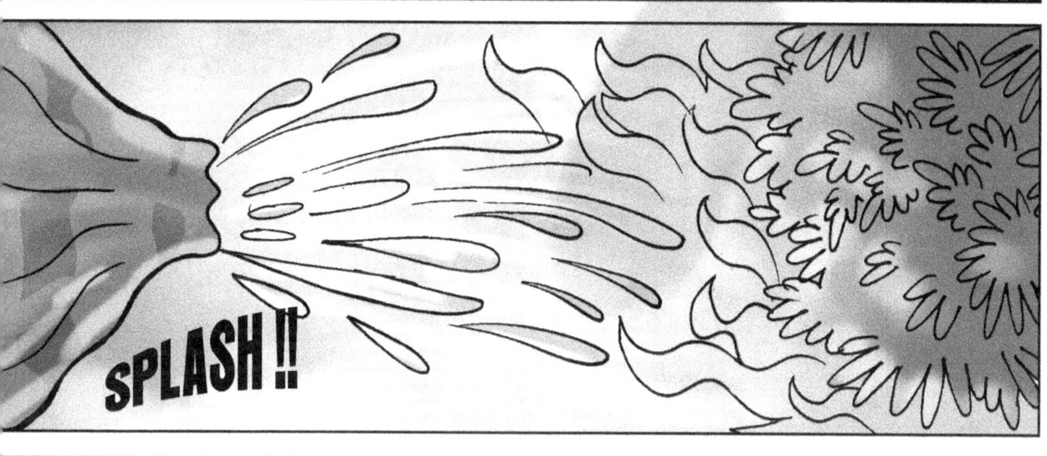

SPLASH!!

THE FOREST FIRE IS GONE.

COME, LET'S ENJOY THE JUNGLE SAFARI.

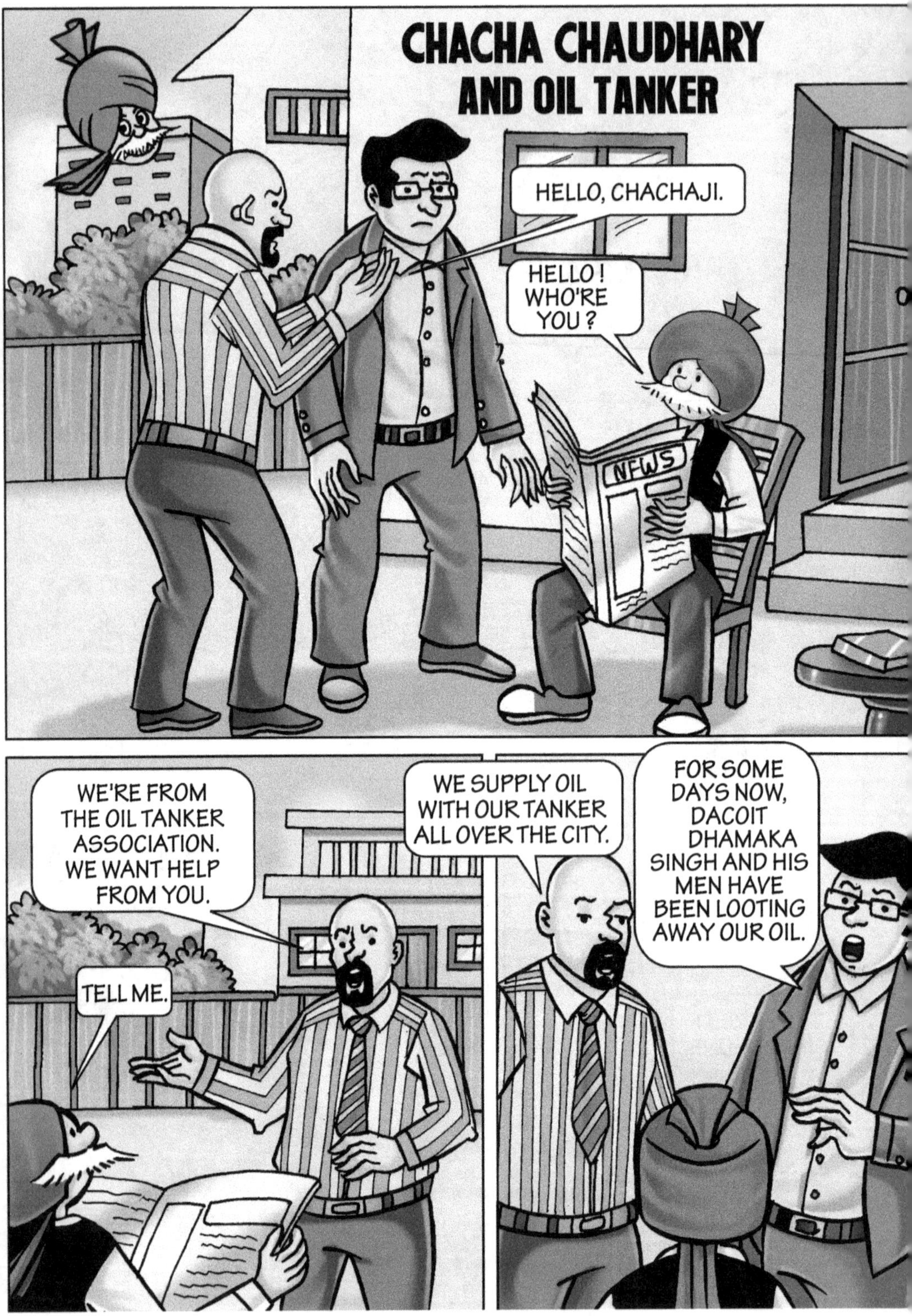

CHACHA CHAUDHARY AND OIL TANKER

WHY DIDN'T YOU REPORT TO THE POLICE ?
WE DID. BUT COULDN'T FIND A SOLUTION.
ONLY YOU CAN SAVE US.
OK.
TODAY I'LL TAKE THE OIL TANKER MYSELF.
OIL TANK
www.chachachaudhary.com

HERE COMES OUR BOOTY.
OIL TANK

HE WON'T GO ANYWHERE. FOLLOW HIM.

STOP ! ELSE WE'LL BLOW AWAY YOUR TANKER.

I DON'T INTEND TO STOP.

THUD !!

ZOOM !!

OH ! THERE'S OIL ON THE ROAD. WAIT.

THERE'S NO TIME TO WAIT NOW. OH !
ZOOMM !!

ZOOMM !!

BANG !

OH GOD !

DO YOU NEED MORE OIL DHAMAKA SINGH ? TAKE IT...
CHACHA CHAUDHARY!

WHY DIDN'T I REALIZE THAT THIS COULD BE NONE OTHER THAN CHACHA CHAUDHARI ?

TOOK YOU A LONG TIME.

BUT NOW WHAT !! IT'S TOO LATE NOW.

THUD !!

HAND THEM OVER TO THE POLICE.
THANKS CHACHAJI!

CHACHA
CHAUDHARY
AND DACOITS
OF THE DESERT

HOW WOULD YOU LIKE TO DIE ? BY THE BULLET OR BY HUNGER AND THIRST IN THE DESERT?

DO YOU KNOW WHOM YOU'RE TALKING TO ? CHACHA CHAUDHARY. HE'S RESPECTED BY THE ENTIRE WORLD.

CHAUDHARY ! I'VE HEARD YOUR NAME A LOT. NOW YOU'LL KISS MY FEET.

YOU PEST ! I'LL BREAK YOUR LEGS.

SABU ! HAVE PATIENCE ! WE CAN'T THINK LOGICALLY WHEN WE'RE ANGRY. LET ME DO WHAT HE SAYS.
www.chachachaudhary.com

CHACHA CHAUDHARY QUICKLY BOW DOWN. ELSE...

OH ! SAND IN MY EYES...

IF ANYONE COMES CLOSER, I'LL SHOOT YOUR CAPTAIN.
?!

YOU'LL TELL US THE WAY OUT.
GO TOWARDS THE EAST.

CHACHA
CHAUDHARY
AND JEWELLERY

YOU'VE NEVER PURCHASED ANY JEWELLERY FOR ME.

BECAUSE I LOVE YOU A LOT.
MEANS ?

DACOITS WILL KILL YOU TO TAKE ALL THE JEWELLERY AWAY.
www.chachachaudhary.com

YOUR EXCUSES WON'T WORK NOW. I'M GOING TO MY MOM'S PLACE.

CHACHAJI ! WHY DIDN'T YOU STOP CHACHI ?

LET HER GO, SABU. WE'RE FREE NOW. THE TROUBLE'S GONE.

TROUBLE HASN'T GONE, BUT DOUBLED UP. CHACHI IS COMING BACK WITH HER MOM.

YOU TROUBLED MY DAUGHTER?

NOW TILL THE TIME YOU DON'T PURCHASE JEWELLERY, I'LL BE RIGHT HERE.

CHACHA CHAUDHARY AND ROCKET

SIR, BE CAREFUL. DON'T BANG INTO MY DOG.
THANKS. I WANT TO MEET CHACHA CHAUDHARY. WILL YOU TAKE ME TO HIM?
IT SEEMS YOU CAN'T SEE.

THE ONE YOU'RE SEARCHING FOR IS RIGHT HERE.
LET ME TOUCH YOUR TURBAN AND BE ASSURED.

WHY DID YOU WANT TO MEET ME ?
I'VE GOT ONE LAKH RUPEES. I WANT TO DONATE THAT TO AN ORPHANAGE.

WILL YOU TAKE ME THERE ?
MY ROCKET WILL TAKE YOU THERE SAFELY.
??

WE HAVE TO ROB HIM OFF.
THAT DOG WON'T LET US DO THAT.

FIRST I'LL SHOOT THE DOG.

BANG !
OH ! I MISSED IT. THERE ARE STILL 5 BULLETS LEFT.

OUCHH !
RUN !
WOOF! WOOF!

GRRRR !
PLEASE FORGIVE ME.

CHACHA CHAUDHARY'S HOUSE

WE'LL STAY IN AGRA FOR A WEEK.
WE'LL SEE TAJMAHAL THERE.

HOTO! WE WERE SEARCHING FOR A HOUSE. WE'VE GOT IT.
JAKALO! HOW'LL WE PAY THE RENT?

NO NEED FOR THAT. CHACHA CHAUDHARY'S HOUSE IS VACANT. WE'LL TAKE THAT.

THE ELECTRICITY, WATER & TELEPHONE BILLS OF THE HOUSE.
DO WE NEED TO PAY THEM?
NO, YOU DUMB.

I'LL GO TO THE CORPORATION OFFICE & GET CHAUDHARY'S NAME REPLACED WITH OURS. THEN WE'LL BE THE OWNER OF THIS PROPERTY.

AFTER A WEEK.
YOU CAN'T ENTER HERE. ALL THE BILLS ARE IN MY NAME. NOW I'M THE OWNER.

MY ANGER IS INCREASING.

THUD !!

BANG !!

OH !! THE HOUSE IS SHAKING.
EARTHQUAKE ! RUN OUT !

NOW IF YOU ENTER, I'LL SMASH YOUR BONES.
THERE GO YOUR BILLS.

CHACHA
CHAUDHARY
AND DIAMOND

CHACHA CHAUDHARY! CAN YOU DROP ME TILL THE BANK SAFELY?
WHAT? NOW?
YES!

WHY DO YOU NEED A SECUTRITY MAN?

I'VE TO DEPOSIT THIS DIAMOND IN THE BANK LOCKER.
MY DOG ROCKET WILL TAKE YOU SAFELY.
OK.

ODI! DO YOU KNOW WHAT THAT MAN HAS GOT?
WHAT BODI?
OUR LUCK! A DIAMOND!

BUT THERE'S A DOG TOO.
I'LL SEPARATE THE DOG FROM HIM.

HE'LL SNIFF THE SWEETS AND FOLLOW ME.
?!

OH ! BRICK.

HE'LL TAKE THE ENTIRE SWEETS.

I'LL HIT HIM WITH A STICK AND SNATCH IT.

BOW ! WOW !
OUCH !!

WE REACHED THE BANK SAFELY.